Dog's New Coat

by Margaret Nash

Illustrated by Lisa Williams

W

D0306279

Notes on the series

TIDDLERS are structured to provide support for children who are starting to read on their own. The stories may also be used for sharing with children.

Starting to read alone can be daunting. **TIDDLERS** help by listing the words in the book for a check before reading, and by providing visual support and repeating words and phrases. These books will both develop confidence and encourage reading and rereading for pleasure.

If you are reading this book with a child, here are a few suggestions:

1. Make reading fun! Choose a time to read when you and the child are relaxed and have time to share the story.
2. Talk about the story before you start reading. Look at the cover and the blurb. What might the story be about? Why might the child like it?
3. Look also at the list of words below - can the child tackle most of the words?
4. Encourage the child to retell the story, using the jumbled picture puzzle.
5. Give praise! Remember that small mistakes need not always be corrected.

Here is a list of the words in this story.

Common words:

a	got	the
at	his	to
back	in	too
but	it	was
came	now	went

Other words:

car	left	park
coat	likes	school
dog	new	shop
		spotty

Dog got a new coat.

But it was too spotty.

Dog left it in the shop.

But the coat
came back.

Dog left it in the car.

But the coat
came back.

Dog left it at school.

But the coat
came back.

17

Dog went to
the park.

Dog likes his spotty
coat now!

Puzzle Time

Can you find these pictures in the story?

c

d

Which pages are the
pictures from?

Answers

The pictures come
from these pages:

a. pages 6 and 7

b. pages 18 and 19

c. pages 12 and 13

d. pages 20 and 21

First published in 2010 by
Franklin Watts
338 Euston Road
London
NW1 3BH

Franklin Watts Australia
Level 17/207 Kent Street
Sydney
NSW 2000

Text © Margaret Nash 2010
Illustration © Lisa Williams 2010

The rights of Margaret Nash to be
identified as the author and Lisa Williams
as the illustrator of this Work have been
asserted in accordance with the Copyright,
Designs and Patents Act, 1988.

All rights reserved. No part of this
publication may be reproduced, stored
in a retrieval system, or transmitted in
any form or by any means, electronic,
mechanical, photocopy, recording or
otherwise, without the prior written
permission of the copyright owner.

A CIP catalogue record for this book is
available from the British Library.

ISBN 978 0 7496 9385 5 (hbk)
ISBN 978 0 7496 9397 8 (pbk)

Series Editor: Jackie Hamley
Series Advisor: Catherine Glavina
Series Designer: Peter Scoulding

Printed in China

Franklin Watts is a division of Hachette Children's Books,
an Hachette UK company. www.hachette.co.uk